This
Treasure Cove Story
belongs to

THE BIG FREEZE

A CENTUM BOOK 978-1-913110-12-3
Published in Great Britain by Centum Books Ltd.
This edition published 2020.

3 5 7 9 10 8 6 4 2

Centum Books Ltd, 20 Devon Square, Newton Abbot, Devon, TQ12 2HR, UK.
9/10 Fenian St, Dublin 2, D02 RX24, Ireland.

www.centumbooksltd.co.uk | books@centumbooksltd.co.uk
CENTUM BOOKS Limited Reg. No. 07641486.

A CIP catalogue record for this book is available
from the British Library.

Printed in China.

A Treasure Cove Story

MARVEL

The Big Freeze

Based on the stories by Marvel Comics
By Billy Wrecks
Illustrated by Michael Borkowski and Michael Atiyeh

The Amazing **Spider-Man** was swinging through New York City when his spider-sense started tingling. 'There's trouble in the park and, as usual, it's headed *my* way,' Spider-Man said. 'I wonder who it will be today – the Green Goblin? Aliens? Doctor Doom?'

Spider-Man jumped out of the way
as a huge green blur hurtled past him.
Now I know there's trouble! Spider-Man thought.

GRRR!

The big green blur smashed into the street. It was the Incredible **Hulk**.

'Now Hulk is angry,' the green giant growled. 'Make Hulk want to **SMASH!**'

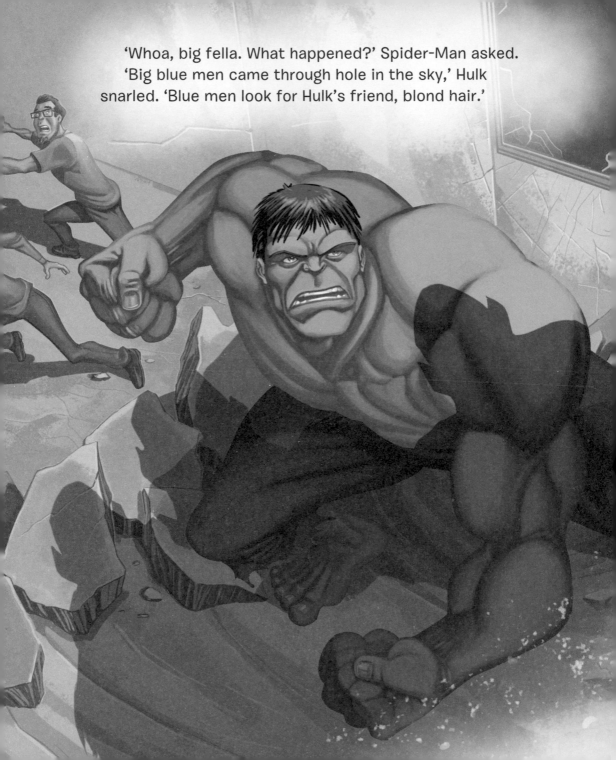

'Whoa, big fella. What happened?' Spider-Man asked.
'Big blue men came through hole in the sky,' Hulk
snarled. 'Blue men look for Hulk's friend, blond hair.'

'Blue men? Blond hair? What are you talking about?'
Spider-Man replied as enormous shadows loomed over
them. 'And why is it getting dark? Uh-oh.'

Spider-Man looked up. Three fierce **Frost Giants** from the distant realm of Asgard towered above them. 'We are looking for Thor,' boomed the leader of the Frost Giants – who was also the biggest. 'And I will cover this city with ice and snow until he faces us!'

Iron Man!

'Thor is on the way,' Iron Man warned the Frost Giants.
'But until he gets here, you will just have to deal with...

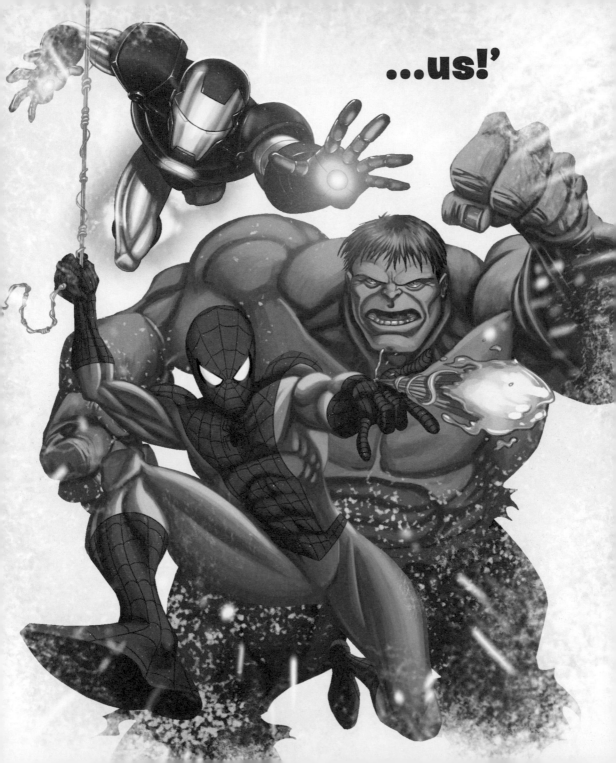

As the biggest Frost Giant continued to summon more snow, Iron Man, Spider-Man and Hulk bravely fought the foes. But the Frost Giants were very big and very strong!

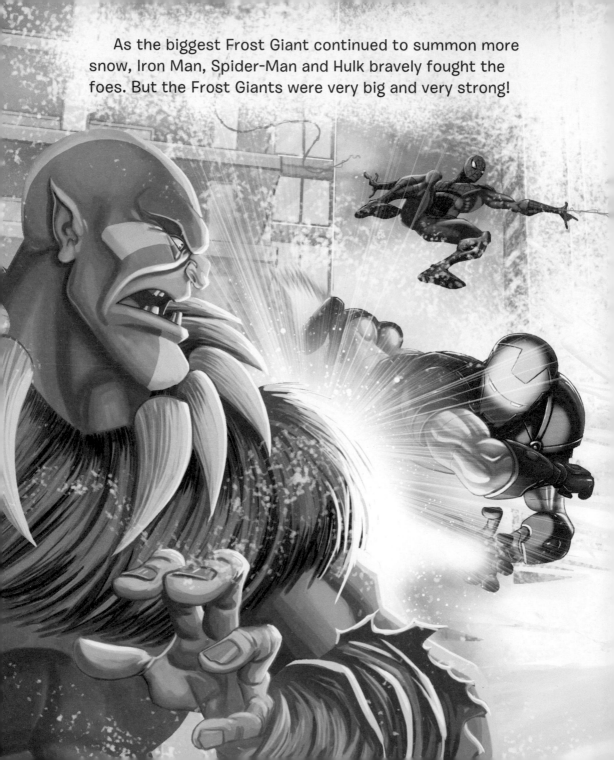

'I thought the bigger they were, the harder they fell!' Spider-Man joked.

'Less talk. More SMASH, Bug Man!' Hulk growled.

'*Brrr*,' Spider-Man said, covering the biggest Frost Giant
with his web. 'You'd better wrap up before you catch a cold.'

'Let's lead the Frost Giants back to the park, where they won't cause as much damage,' Iron Man suggested.

'Good idea, Shell Head,' Spider-Man replied. 'Hulk said something about a hole in the sky. Maybe it's the portal they came through.'

Suddenly, thunder rumbled and lightning flashed!
'Laufey!' **Thor** roared at the biggest Frost Giant.
'What is the meaning of this?'

'The last time we met, on that snowy battlefield, you were victorious,' Laufey snarled. 'I promised to get even. And today I shall!'

Without warning, Laufey hurled a big, frosty snowball at Thor with blinding speed!

Thor swung his mighty hammer and smashed the snowball.
Ice splattered everywhere!

SPLAT!

'**Gotcha!**' Laufey roared gleefully. Then all three
Frost Giants dashed for the open portal in the sky.

'HA! HA!' Thor laughed heartily. 'Well struck, Frost Giants! But this time I have my friends. Join me, heroes!'

The heroes quickly jumped into the snowball fight
with the Frost Giants. Even the people of New York helped!
Thor chased the Frost Giants back to their portal.
As it closed behind them, everyone cheered!

'The Frost Giants are gone, but the city is still covered in snow,' Spider-Man said to Hulk and Iron Man. 'I guess there's only one thing to do – **DUCK!**'

Treasure Cove Stories

Please contact Centum Books to receive the full list of titles in the *Treasure Cove Stories* series. books@centumbooksltd.co.uk

1 Three Little Pigs
2 Snow White and the Seven Dwarfs
3 The Fox and the Hound - Hide-and-Seek
4 Dumbo
5 Cinderella
6 Cinderella's Friends
7 Alice in Wonderland
8 Mad Hatter's Tea Party from Alice in Wonderland
9 Mickey Mouse and his Spaceship
10 Peter Pan
11 Pinocchio
12 Mickey and the Beanstalk
13 Sleeping Beauty and the Good Fairies
14 The Lucky Puppy
15 Chicken Little
16 The Incredibles
17 Coco
18 Winnie the Pooh and Tigger
19 The Sword in the Stone
20 Mary Poppins
21 The Jungle Book
22 Aristocats
23 Lady and the Tramp
24 Bambi
25 Bambi - Friends of the Forest
26 Pete's Dragon
27 Beauty and the Beast - The Teapot's Tale
28 Monsters, Inc. – M is for Monster
29 Finding Nemo
30 The Incredibles 2
31 The Incredibles – Jack-Jack Attack
33 Wall-E
34 Up
35 The Princess and the Frog
36 Toy Story – The Pet Problem

39 Spider-Man – Night of the Vulture!
40 Wreck it Ralph
41 Ralph Breaks the Internet
42 The Invincible Iron Man – Eye of the Dragon
45 Toy Story – A Roaring Adventure
46 Cars – Deputy Mater Saves the Day!
47 Spider-Man – Trapped by the Green Goblin
49 Spider-Man – High Voltage!
50 Frozen
51 Cinderella is my Babysitter
52 Beauty and the Beast - I am the Beast
56 I am a Princess
57 The Big Book of Paw Patrol
58 Paw Patrol - Adventures with Grandpa!
59 Paw Patrol - Pirate Pups!
60 Trolls
61 Trolls Holiday
63 Zootropolis
64 Ariel is my Babysitter
65 Tiana is my Babysitter
66 Belle is my Babysitter
67 Paw Patrol - Itty-Bitty Kitty Rescue
68 Moana
70 Guardians of the Galaxy
71 Captain America - High-Stakes Heist!
72 Ant-Man
73 The Mighty Avengers
74 The Mighty Avengers - Lights Out!
75 The Incredible Hulk
78 Paw Patrol - All-Star Pups!
80 I am Ariel
82 Jasmine is my Babysitter
87 Beauty and the Beast - I am Belle
88 The Lion Guard - The Imaginary Okapi
89 Thor - Thunder Strike!
90 Guardians of the Galaxy - Rocket to the Rescue!
93 Olaf's Frozen Adventure
95 Trolls - Branch's Bunker Birthday

96 Trolls - Poppy's Party
97 The Ugly Duckling
98 Cars - Look Out for Mater!
99 101 Dalmatians
100 The Sorcerer's Apprentice
101 Tangled
102 Avengers – The Threat of Thanos
105 The Mighty Thor
106 Doctor Strange
107 Captain Marvel
108 The Invincible Iron Man
110 The Big Freeze
111 Ratatouille
112 Aladdin
113 Aladdin - I am the Genie
114 Seven Dwarfs Find a House
115 Toy Story
116 Toy Story 4
117 Paw Patrol - Jurassic Bark!
118 Paw Patrol - Mighty Pup Power!
121 The Lion King - I am Simba
122 Winnie the Pooh - The Honey Tree
123 Frozen II
124 Baby Shark and the Colours of the Ocean
125 Baby Shark and the Police Sharks!
126 Trolls World Tour
127 I am Elsa
128 I am Anna
129 I am Olaf
130 I am Mulan
131 Sleeping Beauty
132 Onward
133 Paw Patrol – Puppy Birthday to You!
134 Black Widow
135 Trolls – Poppy's Big Day!
136 Baby Shark and the Tooth Fairy
137 Baby Shark – Mummy Shark
138 Inside Out
139 The Prince and the Pauper
140 Finding Dory
142 The Lion King - Simba's Daring Rescue

Book list may be subject to change. Not all titles are listed.